SPOT A DOG

A DORLING KINDERSLEY BOOK

For Henry

First published in Great Britain in 1995
by Dorling Kindersley Limited,
9 Henrietta Street, London, WC2E 8PS

A CIP catalogue record for this book is
available from the British Library.

ISBN 0-7513-5335-3

Colour reproduction by G.R.B. Graphica, Verona
Printed in Italy by L.E.G.O.

SPOT A DOG

Selected by Lucy Micklethwait

DORLING KINDERSLEY

LONDON • NEW YORK • STUTTGART

I can see
a big dog.

Madame Charpentier and her Children Auguste Renoir

Where is the little dog?

A Woman at her Toilet Jan Steen

Let's find a dappled dog.

"Have a nice day, Mr. Hockney" Peter Blake

Can you spot a dog?

The Cherry Tart Pierre Bonnard

I can see a fluffy dog.

The Prince of Wales's Phaeton George Stubbs

Can you see a shy dog?

The Dancing Class Edgar Degas

Let's find a hungry dog.

The Last Supper French

Can you
spot a dog?

The Peasant Wedding Pieter Bruegel the Elder

I can see a black dog.

Group of People L.S. Lowry

Can you see a white dog?

The Country Outing Fernand Léger

Let's find a flat dog.

Three Musicians Pablo Picasso

Can you spot a dog?

Tobias and the Angel Attributed to Andrea del Verrocchio

Here there is a big dog,
And over there a little dog,
But let's find a leopard
and a camel and a cow.
Can you spot the monkeys?
Do you see the donkey?
What shall we look for now?

Adoration of the Magi Gentile da Fabriano

Picture List

I can see a big dog.
Auguste Renoir 1841-1919, French
*Madame Charpentier and
her Children* 1878
oil on canvas
153.7 x 190.2 cm
Metropolitan Museum of Art,
New York
Catharine Lorillard Wolfe Collection

Where is the little dog?
Jan Steen 1626-1679, Dutch
A Woman at her Toilet 1663
oil on panel
64.7 x 53 cm
Royal Collection, St. James's Palace,
London

Let's find a dappled dog.
Peter Blake b. 1932, British
"Have a nice day, Mr. Hockney"
1981-85
oil on canvas
97.8 x 123.8 cm
Tate Gallery, London

Can you spot a dog?
Pierre Bonnard 1867-1947, French
The Cherry Tart 1908
oil on canvas
115 x 123 cm
Private Collection

I can see a fluffy dog.
George Stubbs 1724-1806, British
The Prince of Wales's Phaeton 1793
oil on canvas
102.2 x 128.3 cm
Royal Collection, St. James's Palace,
London

Can you see a shy dog?
Edgar Degas 1834-1917, French
The Dancing Class 1874
oil on canvas
85 x 75 cm
Musée d'Orsay, Paris

Let's find a hungry dog.
French, School of Picardie, 15th century
The Last Supper from the Thuison-
les-Abbeville Altarpiece c.1480
oil on panel
117.2 x 50.9 cm
Art Institute of Chicago
Mr. and Mrs. Martin A. Ryerson
Collection

Can you spot a dog?
Pieter Bruegel the Elder b. c.1525,
d. 1569, Netherlandish
The Peasant Wedding c.1567
oil on panel
114 x 163 cm
Kunsthistorisches Museum, Vienna

I can see a black dog.
L.S. Lowry 1887-1976, British
Group of People 1959
watercolour
35.5 x 25.4 cm
Salford Museum and Art Gallery, Salford

Can you see a white dog?
Fernand Léger 1881-1955, French
The Country Outing 1954
oil on canvas
245 x 300 cm
Fondation Maeght, Saint-Paul

Let's find a flat dog.
Pablo Picasso 1881-1973, Spanish
Three Musicians 1921
oil on canvas
200.7 x 222.9 cm
Museum of Modern Art, New York
Mrs. Simon Guggenheim Fund

Can you spot a dog?
Attributed to Andrea del Verrocchio
c.1435-1488, Italian
Tobias and the Angel c.1470-80
tempera on wood
84 x 66 cm
National Gallery, London

Here there is a big dog, …
Gentile da Fabriano c.1370-1427,
Italian
Adoration of the Magi 1423
tempera on panel
300 x 282 cm
Uffizi, Florence

Front Cover
The Cherry Tart (detail), Pierre
Bonnard
Spine
Group of People (detail), L.S. Lowry
Half-title page
The Last Supper (detail), French
Imprint page
*Madame Charpentier and her
Children* (detail), Auguste Renoir

Title page
The Peasant Wedding, Pieter Bruegel
the Elder
Picture List
The Dancing Class (detail),
Edgar Degas
Adoration of the Magi (detail),
Gentile de Fabriano

Acknowledgments

The publisher would like to thank the
following for their kind permission to
reproduce the photographs:

The Last Supper, Photograph © 1994, The Art Institute
of Chicago. All rights reserved: **1 (detail), 17**
The Country Outing, Fondation Maeght, Saint-Paul,
France © DACS 1995: **23**
The Peasant Wedding, Kunsthistorisches Museum,
Vienna: **3, 19**
The Dancing Class, Louvre, Paris © photo RMN: **15,
30 (detail)**
Madame Charpentier and her Children, Copyright
© 1994 by the Metropolitan Museum of Modern Art,
Wolfe Fund, 1907: **2 (detail), 5**
Three Musicians, Fontainebleau, Summer 1921,
Photograph © 1995 The Museum of Modern Art, New
York © DACS 1995: **25**

Group of People, City of Salford Museums and Art
Gallery, Salford © Lowry estate: **spine (detail), 21**
Tobias and the Angel, The National Gallery, London: **27**
The Cherry Tart, Private Collection © ADAGP/
SPADEM, Paris and DACS, London 1995: **front cover
(detail), 11**
A Woman at her Toilet, The Royal Collection © Her
Majesty Queen Elizabeth II: **7**
The Prince of Wales's Phaeton, The Royal Collection
© Her Majesty Queen Elizabeth II: **13**
"Have a nice day, Mr. Hockney", The Tate Gallery,
London © Peter Blake: **9**
Adoration of the Magi, Uffizi, Florence. Photo
SCALA: **29, 31 (detail)**